This edition published by Parragon Books Ltd in 2016

Parragon Books Ltd
Chartist House
15–17 Trim Street
Bath BA1 1HA, UK
www.parragon.com

ISBN 978-1-4748-5731-4

Printed in China

PUPS
SAVE THE
PENGUINS

Bath · New York · Cologne · Melbourne · Delhi
Hong Kong · Shenzhen · Singapore

Cap'n Turbot has spent the afternoon out on the bay, watching Wally the walrus perform tricks.

He wants to reward Wally, but when the captain goes to fetch a fish, the bucket is empty!

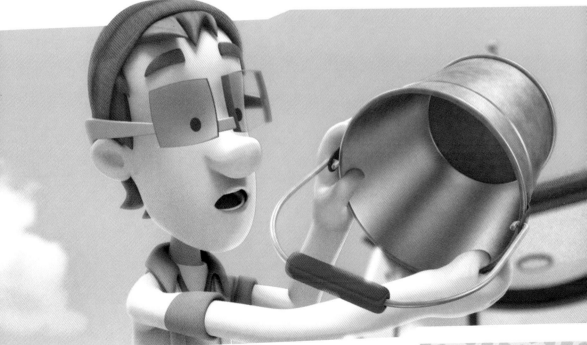

"That's strange," Cap'n Turbot says.
"That bucket was full of fish."

The captain then looks for his tuna
sandwich to give to Wally, but that
is missing, too.

Cap'n Turbot quickly calls Ryder.
He needs the PAW Patrol's help
to solve this mystery.

"Some sinister sneak has been swiping the seafood,"
Cap'n Turbot tells Ryder. "Can you help us find the thief?"

"We'll try our best," Ryder replies. "No job is too big, no pup is too small!"

He activates the PupPad alarm and calls the PAW Patrol to the Lookout.

When they arrive, the pups line up, ready for action.

"All the seafood on Cap'n Turbot's boat has vanished," Ryder explains. "We need to find out who has stolen it and stop them."

Ryder needs Chase's detective skills and Zuma's water gear to help solve the case.

Let's dive in!

On board the Flounder, Zuma explains how they plan to catch the thief. "We'll use these fish-flavoured pup treats as bait," he says.

Then Ryder notices one of the pup treats is missing.

"Somebody took one from right under our noses," he gasps. "Chase, can you pick up the scent?"

"I'll super-sniff them out," Chase barks.

Sniff, sniff!

"What's the smell, Chase?" asks Zuma.

"Fish, fish and more fish ..." says Chase, "... and something I've never smelled before."

He uses his wall-walkers to climb up the side of the cabin and get a better view of the ocean.

"You keep looking up there, Chase," says Ryder.
"Zuma and I will check down below."

They dive into the water with one of the fishy treats.

As Ryder and Zuma search under the boat, a black flipper snatches the treat from Ryder's hand without him seeing.

Ryder and Zuma return to the boat empty-handed.

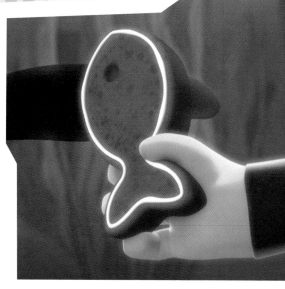

Back on deck, it's starting to get dark. Chase uses his night vision goggles to search for the thief.

He sees some footprints on the deck leading to the trapdoor. Chase follows the trail.

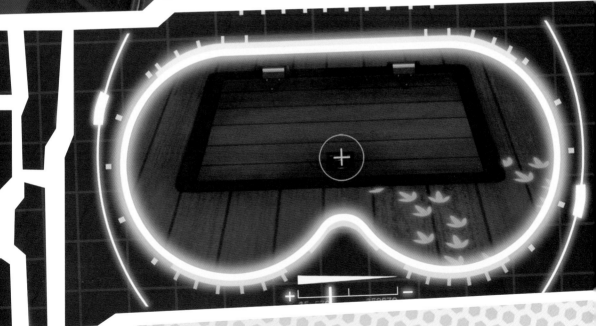

Chase flings open the trapdoor and sees something strange in the dark room.

"Gotcha!" says Chase, sure it's the thief.

But when Ryder appears and turns on the light, the strange shape doesn't belong to the culprit. It belongs to Cap'n Turbot's Driftwood Ducky!

"Let's set a trap," says Ryder.
"We'll put fish treats on the
deck to lure the thief out."

"Spy Chase is on the case!"
the pup barks.

Chase puts the fish treats on the deck and waits up in the cabin. He's shocked when he sees a penguin running towards the treat bucket!

Suddenly, two more penguins appear.

Chase uses his zipline to catch the penguins but misses and falls head first into the bucket.

"Ryder, our slippery suspects are penguins!" Chase reports. "I almost had them but they got away."

"Let's spread out and
search," Ryder tells everyone.

But the cheeky penguins
are too fast to catch!

"We need to get those birds back to their cold home," says Cap'n Turbot. "But how?"

Wally the walrus points to a big iceberg floating past.

"The penguins must have ridden the iceberg here," Ryder says. "Maybe they can ride it back home."

They use Cap'n Turbot's squid snacks to get the penguins' attention.

Zuma uses his hovercraft to drag a bucket of bait onto the iceberg. "Dinner time, little penguins!"

The penguins quickly follow Zuma onto the iceberg.

"They need to get back to colder water – and fast!" warns Cap'n Turbot.

"I've got it!" says Ryder. "Cap'n, let's check your lighthouse log for any ships heading south. We can send the iceberg with them."

"There's a big ship heading to South America," replies Cap'n Turbot.

"Time to move an iceberg!" says Ryder.

The PAW Patrol attach the iceberg to the Flounder, which tugs it to the big ship.

The other pups don't want to miss out on meeting
the penguins, so they all come to play on the iceberg.

"Let's slide like the penguins," Chase tells the pups.
"Just hop up and ride on your belly."

It's soon time for the penguins to go home.
Ryder and the pups hop back on board the Flounder,
and wave goodbye to their penguin friends.

"Good work, pups," says Ryder. "We saved the
day – the PAW Patrol way!"